THE FAIRGROUND GHOST

Felicity Everett

Designed by Maria Wheatley and Alex de Wolf

Illustrated by Alex de Wolf

Language and Reading Consultant: David Wray
(Education Department, University of Exeter, England)

Series Editor: Gaby Waters

First published in 1995 by Usborne Publishing Ltd, Usborne House, 83-85 Saffron Hill, London EC1N 8RT, England.
Printed in Portugal. UE. First published in America March 1996.

One day Jake Hubbard saw a poster on his way to school.

The next day was Saturday.

So Jake asked the dreaded Marcia.
How about you Marcia?
Hmmm, I'll just make a call.
Marcia phoned her boyfriend, the Hunk.
Ok, we'll take you, pest.
Brad the (Hunk)
Grant (slime ball)
What is the Hunk's real name?

They walked into the fairground.

Lights flashed.

Twenty different pop songs blared out at once.

Marcia and the Hunk made straight for the Tunnel of Love.

Jake wanted something scary.

Which ride do you think he chose?

Jake found the ghost train soon enough.
It was a pretty scary ride.
In fact,
his goose bumps
were getting goose bumps...
...until the train went
around the final bend.

WHOOOOO
This was the funniest thing Jake had ever seen.
GHOST INSPECTOR
That little ghost was funny.
A funny ghost? Tell me more.
What does the man with the clipboard do ?

So the ghost train owner called for the little ghost.

Jake was beginning to wish he hadn't laughed.

The little ghost tried its hardest to be scary.

Can you see what score the ghost got?

Off with you.
And don't come back
until you can scare the
fangs off a vampire.
HELP!
TERRIFYING
VERY SCARY
SCARY
The little ghost started
to glide sadly away.
Jake ran after it.
Don't be sad.
Let's go and
have some fun.

At this the little ghost cheered up.
But not for long.

On the merry-go-round,
it was scared to death.

Can you see why?

The little ghost thought the roller coaster looked fine...

...until the ride started.

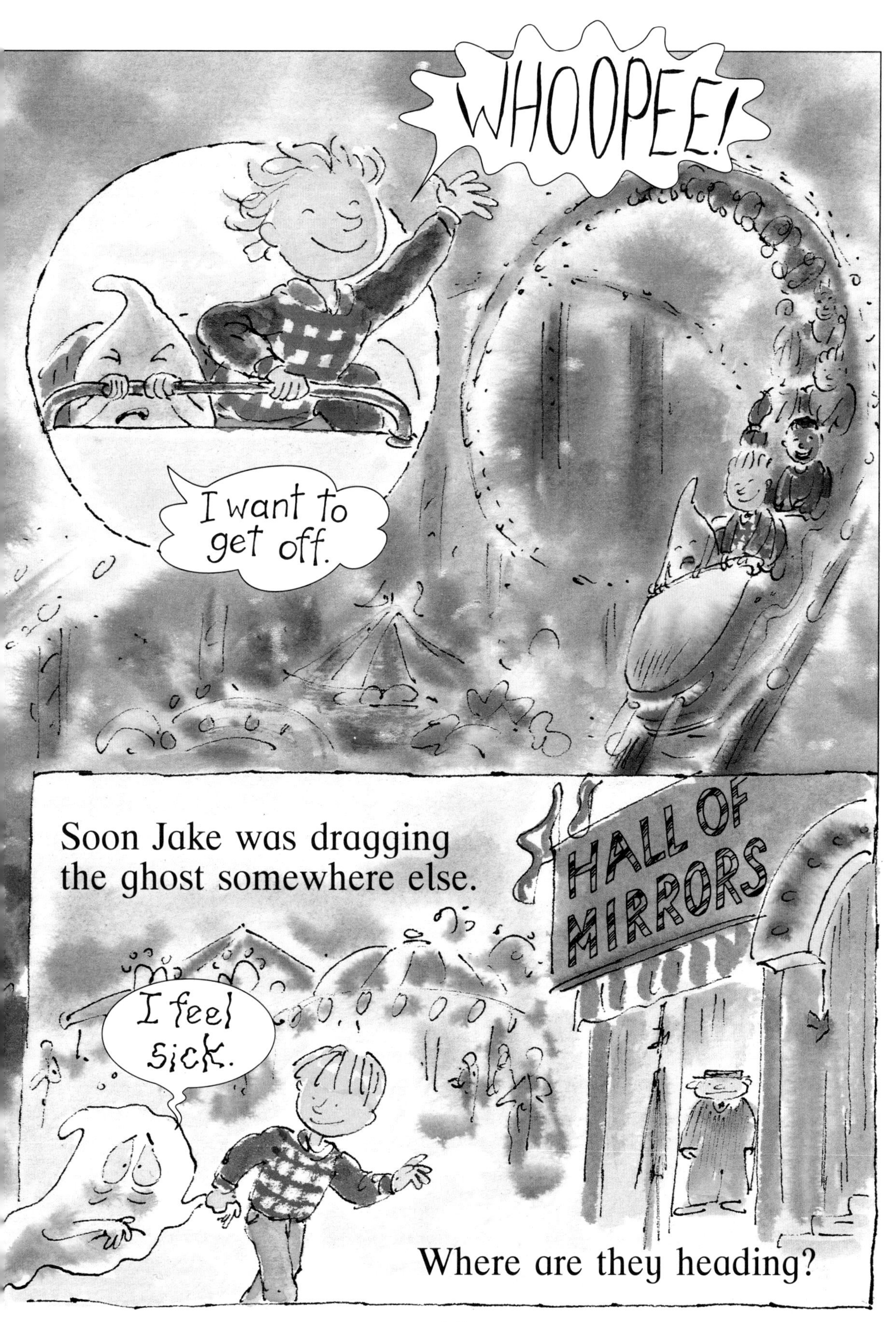

Soon Jake was dragging the ghost somewhere else.

Where are they heading?

Jake told the little ghost to close its eyes and take his hand.

screamed the little
ghost as it caught sight
of its own reflection.

It rushed out,
wailing at the top of its voice.

The eerie howls of the little ghost could be heard in every corner of the fairground.

People scattered.

Stall holders ran for cover.

WHAAA!
Shooting Gallery
Let's get out of here, Brad.
Everyone was terrified, except Jake...
...and someone else.
Can you see who that is?

Jake ran after
the little ghost,
begging it to wait.

The little ghost stopped suddenly.

But Jake was wasting his time.

Why can't the man hear anything?

Jake pleaded with the man to test the ghost on the scare-o-meter again.
Okay, but he doesn't seem any different to me.
Just do what you did in the Hall of Mirrors.
GHOST INSPECTOR
NOT A BIT SCARY
A LITTLE SCARY
SCARY
VERY SCARY
TERRIFYING
HELP!
SCARE-O-METER

Even the ghost inspector had to admit that the little ghost was terrifying.
GHOST INSPECTOR
NOT A BIT SCARY
SCARY
VERY SCARY
TERRIFYING
HELP!
He can take Dracula's place.
Fangs a lot!
GHOST INSPECTOR
Visit Dentist 2 o'clock
Where was Dracula off to?

After that, the ghost train became the busiest ride in the whole fairground.

People came off with their knees knocking and their knuckles white...

...and then went back for another turn.

As for Jake, he got every ride free, thanks to his friend the fairground ghost.